This book is a presentation of Newfield Publications, Inc.
Newfield Publications offers book clubs for children from preschool through high school.
For further information write to: **Newfield Publications, Inc.,**
4343 Equity Drive, Columbus, Ohio 43228.

Published by arrangement with Houghton Mifflin Company.
Newfield Publications is a trademark of Newfield Publications, Inc.
Weekly Reader is a federally registered trademark of
Weekly Reader Corporation.
Printed in the United States of America.

Library of Congress Cataloging-in-Publication Data
Alborough, Jez.
Beaky/Jez Alborough
p. cm.
"First published in Great Britain in 1990
by Walker Books"—T.p.verso
Summary: An egg tumbles to the forest floor and hatches, but its offspring doesn't know
what kind of animal it is until a frog helps it on a quest for identity.
ISBN 0-395-53348-1
[1. Identity— Fiction. 2. Birds—Fiction. 3. Animals—Fiction.] I. Title
PZ7.A323Be   1990   89-39862
[E]—dc20   CIP
                     AC

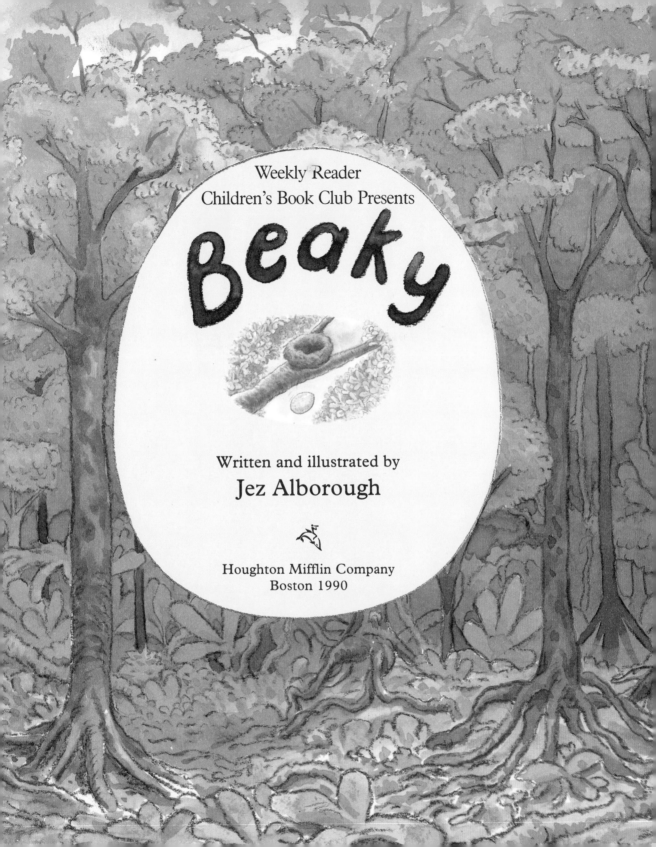

Weekly Reader
Children's Book Club Presents

Beaky

Written and illustrated by
Jez Alborough

Houghton Mifflin Company
Boston 1990

An egg tumbled down through the leaves and branches
and shattered into pieces on the rain forest floor.

Out popped a fluffy creature

    with a bright blue beak

        and a curly orange tail.

"Hello," croaked Frog, jumping out from behind a bush.

"I'm a frog, what are you?"

The creature looked confused.

"Don't you know what you are?" asked Frog.

The creature shook its head.

"Then you can be my friend," said Frog.

"I will call you Beaky. Come on, let's go for a walk."

"Am I a frog?" asked Beaky as they hopped along.

Frog laughed. "If you were a frog," he said,

"then you would be able to hop as high as me

and you wouldn't have those funny fluffy flaps."

"If I'm not a frog," said Beaky, "then what am I?"
"I don't know," puzzled Frog, "I've never
seen anything like you before; but you must be
something . . . everything is something!"

Before long they found Snake.

"What's he doing?" asked Beaky.

"Slithering," said Frog.

"Precisely," said Snake. "It's simply
splendid to slither, you should try
a slither yourself."

"Yes, try it," said Frog, for he
wondered whether Beaky might
be some sort of snake.
So Beaky lay
on the earth
and tried
to slither.
Nothing happened.
"Oh dear," said Frog.
Snake laughed. "Too short," he said,
and slithered off into the trees.

Beaky and Frog hopped to the river where they
found Fish gliding about in the water.

"What's he doing?" asked Beaky.

"I'm swimming," said Fish. "Come and join me,
  the water's lovely."

"Good idea," said Frog, thinking that Beaky
  might be some sort of fish. "Try a swim."

Beaky splished and splashed and flipped
and flapped, but couldn't swim a stroke.
"Oh dear," said Frog.
Fish giggled. "Too fluffy," he said,
and swam away.

"Everyone knows what he is except me,"
sighed Beaky.

Just then he heard something singing softly, far away.

"Did you hear that?" he asked excitedly.

"Hear what?" said Frog.

"Listen!" said Beaky. "It came from up there."

Frog looked up to the top of the trees, then he
heard it too.

"Someone up there must be really happy," said Beaky,
"to sing such a joyful song. Do you think I could
ever be that happy?"

"Maybe," said Frog, "but not until we discover what
you are."

Then he had an idea. "Let's climb up there,"
he said, "and see if we can find out."

So up they went, but the higher they climbed

the more frightened Frog became.

So Beaky had to go on alone.

On and on he struggled, all through the day and
into the night until he could go no further.

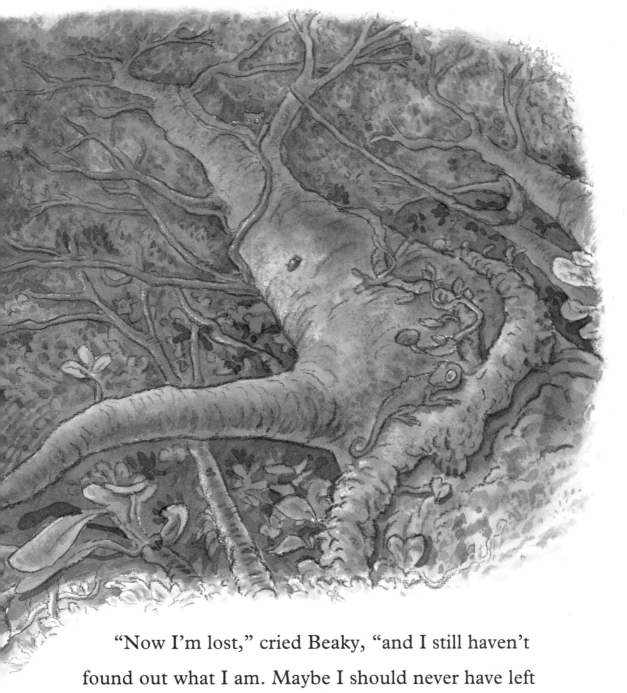

"Now I'm lost," cried Beaky, "and I still haven't found out what I am. Maybe I should never have left the forest floor. Perhaps the song was just a dream." And with this thought, he slept.

Beaky awoke the next morning to
the sound of a familiar song.
Looking around, he saw circling in the air a beautiful
fluffy creature with a bright blue beak and a curly orange tail.

"What are you?" called Beaky.

"I'm a bird," sang the creature, "a bird of Paradise."

"A bird," said Beaky, "that's what I am."

In his excitement he jumped and skipped and dipped,

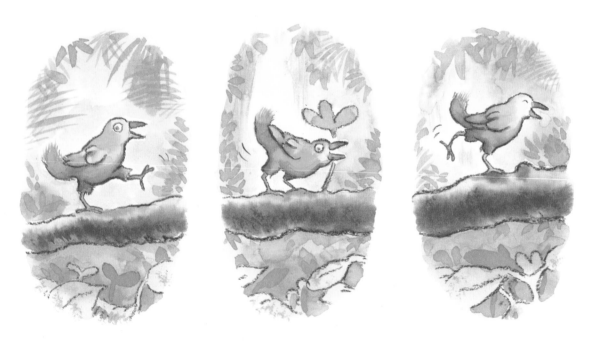

he strutted, bobbed and trotted and then . . .

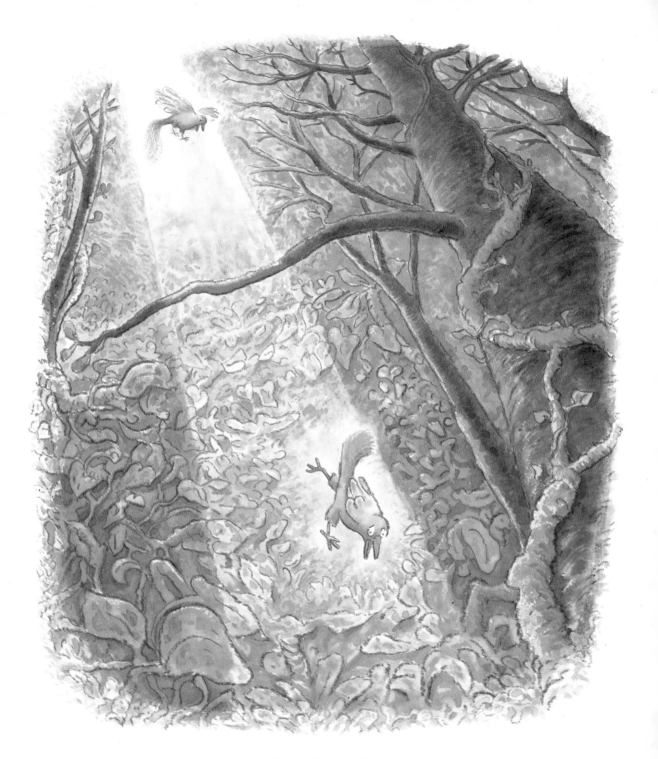

he tripped!

Down
and
down he fell,
crashing through
leaves and branches,
down towards the
earth below.
"Flap your wings!"
called the bird.
"Flap your wings!"
Beaky opened wide
his fluffy flaps.
"My wings," he cried,
"these are my *wings*."
And with a *whoosh*
he began to fly . . .

up past a tree where Snake was slithering . . .

down to the river where Fish was swimming . . .

and back to the vine where Frog was still waiting.

"Frog," said Beaky, "look at me. I can't slither,
or swim, or hop like you, but I can *fly*!"
At that moment Beaky heard the singing
once more and it seemed to be calling him.
"I must go," he said, "but I'll come back and visit."

Then he flew up towards the treetops.

"Beaky," called Frog, "you haven't told me what you are."

"I'm a bird," cried Beaky.

"I'm a bird . . . a bird of Paradise!"